THE UPSIDE-DOWN BOY

Written by Janet Palazzo-Craig
Illustrated by Ray Burns

Troll Associates

Library of Congress Cataloging in Publication Data

Palazzo-Craig, Janet.
    The upside-down boy.

    Summary: Donnie spends his life being upside down
much to the dismay of those who know him, but a day
comes when his unusual stance benefits the town.
    [1. Posture—Fiction] I. Burns, Raymond,
1924-   ill. II. Title.
PZ7.P1762Up   1986   [E]   85-14067
ISBN 0-8167-0604-2 (lib. bdg.)
ISBN 0-8167-0605-0 (pbk.)

10   9   8   7   6   5   4   3   2

THE UPSIDE-DOWN BOY

Donnie was a very good boy.
But there was one little thing
that was different about him.
He liked to be upside down.

It didn't matter where. It didn't
matter when. He just loved
being upside down.

It started when he was a baby.
His mother knew it right away.
She walked into his room. There
he was, standing on his head in
the crib.
"Mama," he said with a smile—
an upside-down smile, of course.

And that was just the beginning.

Did you ever eat your oatmeal upside down? No? Well, Donnie did.

It drove his parents crazy.
"That's not the way to sit at the
table," said his mother.
"You're going to hurt yourself,"
said his father.
Donnie just swallowed his
oatmeal and smiled. His parents
groaned.

Did you ever watch TV upside down? Donnie did. He liked it much better that way.

He watched upside-down horses
gallop across the set. He saw
upside-down monkeys swinging
in upside-down trees. In fact,
everything Donnie saw was
upside down.
He laughed and laughed—
especially at the commercials.

"What's so funny?" asked
Donnie's father.
But Donnie just laughed and
laughed.

A really strange sight was
Donnie walking his dog. All the
neighbors would look out their
windows. Cars would stop
short.

Donnie thought it was fun. His
dog did *not* think it was fun.
"Look at that boy! How
unusual!" everyone said.

"You'd better watch where you're going," said grumpy old Mr. Ticker. "You'd better walk right-side up."

"*Woof, woof,*" added Donnie's dog.

He happened to agree with Mr. Ticker. But Donnie just smiled and kept walking.

At school, it was worse.
Donnie's teacher tried her best.
She certainly sent home enough
notes to Donnie's parents—notes
like this one:

Dear Mr. and Mrs. Green:
Donnie is good.
He's a very smart boy.
But I'm sorry to tell you
that teaching him *isn't* a joy.
Upside down at his desk,
the same way in his chair—
I'm just about ready to pull out
    my hair!
His upside-down reading and
    upside-down writing
make teaching your Donnie
    much more than exciting.
Please talk with your son.
He must learn this rule:
He shouldn't be upside down
when he's in school.
                Sincerely,
                Mrs. Minkey

Even at the playground, there
was upside-down Donnie. He
didn't look so bad on the
monkey bars. He even looked
good swinging from the rings!

20

But then there was baseball.
Now that was a problem.

"You can't play with us,
Donnie," the other kids said.
"No way! How will you ever
catch the ball?"
Donnie had to admit they were
right. Sometimes being upside
down wasn't such a good idea.
But most of the time, Donnie
liked it just fine.

One day, the teacher told them
the good news. There was going
to be a big parade. And their
class was going to be in it.

There'd be music and balloons
and good things to eat!
Everyone cheered. Donnie was
so excited he almost sat right-
side up. That is, until he heard
the bad news.

"Donnie," said Mrs. Minkey,
"you're welcome to be in the
parade. But you can't march
upside down."
Donnie couldn't believe his ears.

"But Mrs. Minkey," he said, "I know how to march upside down. I can keep up with everyone else."

"I'm sorry," said Mrs. Minkey. "You'll just have to march like the other girls and boys."

Donnie wanted to be in the parade. But march right-side up? It just wouldn't be any fun. Donnie guessed he would have to watch the parade instead of being in it.

Finally, the big day came. The whole town was buzzing. What hustle! What bustle!

Costumes were ready to wear.
Batons were ready to twirl.
Music was ready to play. It was
very exciting—for everyone
except Donnie, that is.

"*Toot!*"
Someone blew a whistle.
"*Boom!*"
Someone beat a drum.
And the parade began.

30

Music. Cheering. Singing.
Noises filled the air. And people
filled the sidewalks to watch.

Where was Donnie? Why,
upside down, of course.

He and his dog were in the
crowd. They followed the
parade down the street. It was a
great parade. There was only
one problem. Donnie couldn't
see much of it. And being upside
down didn't make it any easier.

"Darn!" said Donnie. "I can't
see a thing!"
And he was *just* about to turn
himself right-side up when...
suddenly, he stopped.

His eyes grew big.
"*Woof!*" said the dog.
He saw it, too.

In the cellar window, just where no one would ever look (unless they were upside down, of course), Donnie saw robbers. They were filling a bag with money.

Donnie looked at the sign on the building. It said "ʞuɐꓭ."

Donnie sprang to his feet. Now
the sign said "Bank."

Donnie was off. He ran as
quickly as his *feet* could carry
him. He ran straight to the
police officer at the head of the
parade.

"Quick! Come with me! The
bank's being robbed," he
shouted.
The whole parade stopped.
Nobody moved. No one said a
word.

They all stood there looking at
Donnie. They were more than a
little surprised to see upside-
down Donnie standing right-side
up!

"Come on, let's go!" said
Donnie.
And away they all ran down the
street.

Grownups, children, dogs,
police officers, baton twirlers,
fire fighters, and even old Mr.
Ticker rushed as fast as they
could to the bank.

Well, that was the end of those robbers. And it was all thanks to Donnie.

The newspapers told the story:
UPSIDE-DOWN BOY FOILS
THIEVES!

The bank even gave Donnie a
reward.

But the best reward of all was
being able to lead the parade.
Can you guess how he did it?

Upside down, of course!